Gifts

Gifts

A Christmas Novella

JEANETTE HANSCOME

Gifts, a Christmas Novella

Published in association with the Books & Such Literary Management, 52 Mission Circle, Suite 122, PMB 170, Santa Rosa, CA 95409-5370, www.booksandsuch.com.

This story is dedicated to the anonymous friends who gave me and my sons a 12 Days of Christmas box in December 2011.

Chapter 1

It was Target two days before Christmas Eve, so the lack of selection in the gift wrap section hadn't phased me at all. The screaming toddler ahead of me in line for the cashier on the other hand...

His poor mother.

The little guy's wails competed with the newest cover of "Last Christmas." He kicked his legs until one of his Spiderman sneakers flew off. I tried not to stare as his frazzled mother retrieved it and bribed him with organic crackers shaped like bunnies. "Atticus, I need you to listen to Mommy and stop screaming. We get to go right home after this."

She turned to me, her hands frantically shoving Atticus's foot into his shoe. "He missed his nap."

"Poor thing." I gave the mom a sympathetic smile as Atticus tossed a bunny cracker at the gum and mints display. Seeing the impeccably dressed woman squeeze the bridge of her nose to fight back tears chased away a judgy assumption about parents who subject their kids to shopping marathons during the holidays. As an unmarried thirty-one-year-old, I had no idea.

Atticus finally stopped screaming when his mom pulled a battered stuffed octopus out of her giant black purse and handed it to him. She ran her fingers under her eyelids. How embarrassing to start crying in a store.

I tucked the white tissue and curling ribbon I'd settled for under my arm and pretended to be looking through my tote bag for my wallet. Instead I pulled out a bright red envelope and a cellophane goody bag filled with ten foil-wrapped truffles. Exactly ten. The good kind, not the cheap stuff that tastes like essence of foil.

I held the bag behind my purchases until Atticus's mother had paid. What I really wanted to do was slip the goody bag into her purse and let her discover it in the car, but in this festive season of theft, I opted for saying, "Excuse me," and holding it out to her. "This is for you."

Her mouth dropped open. "What?"

I smiled. "Merry Christmas."

Her eyes filled with tears. "Oh my goodness. That's so sweet of you." She examined the bag from all angles. She smiled through her tears. "What's your name?"

"Justine."

"Thank you, Justine."

Atticus reached for the bag. "Whatsat?"

His mom pulled the bag and card to her chest. "It's for Mommy." She hid it safely in her purse.

I made an *It's yucky* face at Atticus. "You wouldn't like it."

He clutched his grinning octopus by one of its legs and looked at me suspiciously.

The woman reached out and squeezed my arm. "You have no idea how much I needed something like this."

I squeezed her arm back. "I'm so glad it helped. Have a wonderful night."

"You, too."

As she walked away, I turned to the cashier, who was looking at me like she wanted to ask, *Do you do that in every checkout line? Will I get chocolate?*

I set my wrapping supplies in front of her. "She looked like she needed a treat."

Ten gifts down, two more to go, and each one got more fun.

"I'm home!" I dropped my tote and shopping bag on the couch. The apartment I shared with my Aunt Sheila was quiet. A stack of mail and a small square package sat on the table, so my aunt had obviously come home after getting off work. Was it book club, choir rehearsal for the Christmas Eve service, dinner with her Happy Single Ladies, or her turn to lead an activity at Sunny Harbor Senior Center where she technically worked as a nurse but couldn't help also volunteering for bingo night and show tune sing-alongs? After almost a decade of living here, keeping track of her active social calendar was still a challenge.

I turned on the Christmas tree lights. Our apartment was not nearly large enough to support the aroma of my aunt's many scented pinecones, real Christmas tree, and live wreath. But I enjoyed it while I could. I'd just spent the day managing the reservation desk at the Main Street Hotel where fear of upsetting a guest's fragrance allergies meant a holiday decked in pretty plastic with only hints of cinnamon.

I plopped into a kitchen chair and started sorting the mail into my pile and Aunt Sheila's. Two Christmas cards and a water bill for Aunt Sheila, a Christmas card from Mom and a credit card application for me. The package had my name on it, hand-written. "Ooh, yes!" I tore the application in half and reached for the package.

I felt giddy inside even though I knew I couldn't open it until Christmas morning. Well, I could. I was a grown woman who could make her own gift rules. But I always waited. Half the fun of the gift-giving part of Christmas was wondering what was in each package.

Then I looked at the return address and the giddiness fizzled.

Now I was the one in need of chocolate.

How did he find my address?

Chapter 2

"Justine, he's your father." Aunt Sheila stood in my bedroom doorway, holding the chef nutcracker that she'd taken from her friend Liz at the Happy Single Ladies annual Christmas dinner and gift exchange the night before.

"Stepfather." At one time I called him Dad, but not anymore.

I detested the side of me that emerged when my mom's second husband, Jason, came up in conversation—the man who duped me and Mom into thinking he wasn't like all the others, the man who solidified my decision to take a vow of lifelong celibacy. I even had a floppy old spinster hat stashed away for future use and pictures of the cats I planned to have as roommates in a tacky-in-a-charming-way tiny house in either the Sierra Foothills or Santa Cruz. I was still too young for eccentric to be considered endearing, but it helped to prepare.

I tied red and green ribbon around the lumpy rectangle wrapped in the white tissue that I'd made less boring by decorated it with holly berry stickers.

"Don't you want to know what he sent?"

"Nope."

I tightened the bow then slipped a small card under it and set the gift aside on my bed. I nestled a small gift bag containing a wrapped mini snow globe, eleven peppermints, and another card into my tote.

The last two presents from my 12 Days of Christmas gift box. I already knew who I planned to give the snow globe to, but the future of the lumpy rectangle remained a mystery.

Aunt Sheila came into my room and sat on my bed. "Will you at least think about it?"

"I already have."

"Why are you being so stubborn?"

"Because I have a feeling that he's trying to suck up." I went in search of my shoes.

"Please don't say suck up, Justine. It's crude, and very out of character for you."

"It's not out of character if I say it." I attempted a snarky sneer, but I could still taste the bitterness of my own words on my tongue. I looked at my aunt but found myself staring at the chef nutcracker instead. "Have you forgotten what he did?"

She propped the nutcracker against my pillows. It fell over with its French-mustache-lined mouth open. "That was so long ago. Your mother has forgiven Jason. Why can't you?"

I shut my plastic container of wrapping supplies and slid it under my bed. "Because he hasn't asked. If he was truly sorry, he would've called me and asked how to make things right before sending a random Christmas present." I flung my tote over my shoulder and rushed to the front door even though I didn't need to be at work for more than half an hour. We both knew I had plenty of time to drive there. It took less than ten minutes to get from our front door to the front desk at the hotel. I saw only one drawback to my life in this small Bay Area city: the apartment that Aunt Sheila and I shared was too conveniently located. Neither of us could avoid unpleasant topics with, "Oh, wow, with traffic and everything, I should really get going."

Sound bites from every sermon and retreat talk about forgiveness came back to me until I finally relented. "I'll think about it."

I dropped a dollar into the tip jar at Full 'a Beans Coffee & Tea and stepped aside to wait for my holiday indulgence. Meg, the girl making my pumpkin spice latte, handed a steaming cup to a woman in alarmingly high heels and snowflake leggings.

I was envying the woman's ability to walk in high heels so gracefully when she said to Meg, "What a pretty pin you have on."

"Thank you." Meg touched the angel on her apron. "It was a gift."

"Your friend has good taste."

I turned toward the clearance table and pretended to be interested in a mug shaped like a snowman's head. Only at Christmastime and at Disneyland would I even consider drinking out of a head.

"The fun part is, I don't even know who gave it to me." Meg lowered her voice a little, but a lilt still came through. "Someone left it for me a few days ago and didn't sign their name. It totally made my day."

Yes! I'd pulled it off.

Meg had received Gift #8. I chose her because she often looked tired while taking my order and talked about juggling school with two jobs. All that, and she still remembered that I liked cinnamon on all my coffee drinks.

"Pumpkin spice latte for Justine," Meg called after exchanging holiday greetings with The Lady in Heels.

I bit my lip to cover the *I have a secret* smile that was trying to escape.

Meg handed me a cinnamon shaker with my latte. "I saw someone swipe the one from the bar and take it to her table."

"Thank you." I gave my drink a good shake of cinnamon and handed the container back to her. Meg's eyes looked bright, not like last week when I popped in for a quick caffeine infusion before work and overheard her tell the other cashier that her boyfriend broke up with her via text. Watching her fight back tears as she prepared a medium roast drip for a man who couldn't get over the inconvenience of standing in line let alone see her pain inspired me to give her the angel pin with four red and green stones on each glittered wing. I'd found it at Rite Aid, but one would never know. It looked perfect on her. I snapped a lid onto my cup. "Are you enjoying the break from classes?"

"So much. I passed that awful statistics class. I've never been so happy to get a 'C' in my life."

"I hated statistics." It had been ten years since I dropped out of school mid-semester, one year short of my Social Work degree, and I still missed college. Even statistics.

I missed Alex, my too-good-to-be-true boyfriend-at-the-time. Why did I always miss him at Christmas? I missed him slipping his leather jacket around my shoulders when I got cold, and the way he gave stink eye to anyone who treated me like less than the Queen. I missed his younger sister, Amy, who treated me like family long before her brother and I were an official couple and pulled me into her friendship circle as soon as she found out we were at the same college. I thought of her when-ever someone overused emojis and dancing cartoon characters on social media. She'd called me in tears after I broke up with her brother. But that's what happens when someone else's choices send you running from nice people, and the campus is too small to avoid bumping into each other.

I swallowed memories of Alex with a swig of cinnamony coffee. It didn't work. "Merry Christmas, Meg."

"Merry Christmas." She smiled at me then greeted her next customer. The stones on her pin sparkled, making her blue-grey eyes gleam. What would Jason's eyes look like when he saw *Return to Sender* stamped across the gift that he'd sent me?

Chapter 3

I sipped the spicy goodness in my cup before pulling out of the Full 'a Beans parking area and considered the gifts I planned to give away—the little snow globe with peppermints today and a pretty ceramic cross with *Grace* painted in gold letters tomorrow, Christmas Eve. The snow globe had my boss Lydia's name on it. She lost her mom at Easter and was struggling through her first holiday season without her. The cross could go to ... who needed it? One of Aunt Sheila's Happy Single Ladies maybe? She was the one person who knew I did this.

I started the 12 Days of Christmas tradition the year after receiving an anonymous box of packages. The year I received the box, I had just thrown my future off the Golden Gate Bridge and moved in with Aunt Sheila because Mom's disappointment was too much to bear. Whoever gave it to me had left it on Mom's porch, then Mom left it on Sheila's. At first, I thought Alex sent it in an attempt to win me back, but the handwriting on the card didn't match his boxy printing.

The instructions said to open one gift per day between December 13 and Christmas Eve. Each package included a card with a Bible verse that left me wondering how this mystery person knew what was going on in my heart that day. None of the presents were anything fancy—a pair of cozy socks on Day 2, a pack of four candy cane-striped pens on Day 4, a half dozen chocolates that happened to be my favorite on Day 6. Then I unwrapped the final gift. Inside a miniature stocking I found half of a sterling silver friendship heart on a chain. The half-heart had a pair of praying hands in the center. The card included twelve verses about God's love for me, and the note, "I promise to pray for you every day." I still wore the heart as a reminder that, even at my lowest, God loved me enough to prompt someone to be that kind. I kept all the cards in a special box in my room. Sometimes I caught myself wondering if the anonymous giver still prayed for me.

The next year I decided to pass the joy on to someone else. I gave the box to an elderly woman in our apartment complex who was battling cancer. Like the gifts I received, my packages contained inexpensive presents and cards with a Bible verse in each one, except for the gift for Christmas Eve, which was extra special. I gave her a Nativity scene ornament because it was known throughout the complex that she collected Nativity scenes. Her card included the same twelve verses that I'd received with my necklace. I had so much fun with my first act of secret giving that I made it a tradition. This year I'd decided to change it up and give each of my twelve gifts to a different person. Most of them went to people I knew just well enough to recognize they needed a lift, like Meg. A few went to strangers, like the frazzled mom in Target.

Tomorrow's gift needed to go to someone who needed a reminder of God's grace and twelve verses about his love as much as Atticus's mother needed chocolate.

My phone chimed as I pulled into the Staff Only parking lot behind the Main Street Hotel. I savored my drink and checked the text, expecting to see one from Aunt Sheila, sharing a story she'd just read online about a man who died—most likely of a broken heart—shortly after sending an estranged loved one a Christmas gift and not getting a response.

Instead it was a number I didn't recognize.

Hello Justine. It's Jason. I know it has been a long time. I hope I have the right number. I sent you a package and just want to confirm that it reached you. Merry Christmas.

My fingers quivered with the impulse to reply while my mind screamed, *Don't.* Getting pulled into a text exchange would only make this harder.

Your mother has forgiven him. Why can't you?

I wiped foamed milk off my lips.

Why couldn't I?

If those who considered me a nice person only knew the truth.

My boss, Lydia, rushed across the lobby to meet me before the jingle bells on the hotel entrance had a chance to stop tinkling. "Good, you're here." She grabbed my arm.

"Am I late?" I checked the garland-draped grandfather clock in the hotel lobby. I still had three minutes.

"No, but we have an emergency."

I glanced at my coffee cup then at my tote bag then at my boss. My heart started to race.

Lydia waved her hand toward the hallway leading to the room that the hotel staff used for breaks. "I'm sorry. You can put your stuff down first."

I gave myself permission to exhale. "Be right back."

When I returned from the break room, Lydia was standing in the entrance to the dining room section of the hotel, which would open for lunch in less than an hour. The aroma of chicken and sage stuffing drifted in from the hotel kitchen. Lydia's hands rested on her once-slender hips as she scanned the empty tables, muttering to herself. After nine years of working with her, I knew this meant that she was trying to figure out how to make the impossible happen.

"What's up?"

She jumped back then put her hands over her eyes for a moment and took a calming breath. "Let's sit down."

We sat on the antique sofa where guests waited for a table when we were extra busy, which wasn't very often anymore.

I pinned my name badge on. "Are you okay?"

"I was until I got a call from Brenda Murray."

"Brenda who?" The name sounded familiar.

"Brenda Murray from yesterday. The woman who called in tears right before you left."

I thought back to the day before. "That's right." How could I forget? I'd answered the phone when a teary woman asked for Lydia and begged her to reserve the restaurant's Garden Room for a family Christmas Eve gathering. Her washing machine hose had burst while she was at work and flooded half the first floor of her upscale home, including the living room, the dining room, and a guest room. Thankfully, the Garden Room was free. She'd also booked two of our nicest suites for out-of-town relatives.

"I thought this reservation was the answer to your Christmas prayers." For the past year, we'd been feeling the strain of competing with an obscene selection of great places to eat, have parties, and spend a night away from home.

"It was." Lydia's voice cracked. "Until today when she called again with *a few little things* regarding tomorrow." Lydia shook her head in theatrical despair. "I have no idea how I'm going to do everything she wants by tomorrow."

Poor Lydia. She'd been emotionally fragile since Thanksgiving. "What were the few little things?"

Lydia pushed back her short gray hair and rubbed her temples. "It's a theme party. With costumes." She impersonated Brenda Murray's voice. "And appropriate décor, of course."

I looked around at the decorations that the Main Street Hotel was so well known for—Victorian from ceiling to floor, regardless of current trends. For Christmas, we went all out with villages, garland, and trees so packed with ornaments that the green was barely visible. Brenda Murray, whoever she was, could not mess with our signature look.

Lydia shook her hands at the ceiling as if the chandelier was the one at fault. "*Grrr.* I've known Brenda since our sons were in kindergarten together. She has always been high maintenance. I drew the line at separate checks and asking the servers to speak in a British accent. They will get the same menu as everyone else who books the Garden Room for a large group during the holidays—three seasonal entrée choices with a vegetarian option and smaller portions for kids, unless they want a snowman-shaped PB&J or chicken tenders."

British accents? What kind of party was this woman throwing? I refrained from spouting off a snotty comment about Bay Area wealth and entitlement, another bad habit that Aunt Sheila considered out of character for a sweet woman like me. Working for Lydia and meeting so many nice guests at this historic hotel had shown me that not everyone with money acted like some of the girls I went to camp with back in my scholarship kid days. "What's the theme?"

"A Christmas Carol."

"As in Dickens?"

She rested her head against the wall behind us. "Yes."

"Who adds something like that at the last minute?"

"Apparently, it was the family's plan all along, but in her distress, Brenda completely forgot to mention it last night."

"What a thing to forget." I shrugged and tried to come up with something to ease Lydia's nerves. "I don't mind helping you work with a Dickens theme. It's not like she expects the staff to wear costumes."

"Funny you should mention that."

Now I was the one who wanted to shake my hands at the ceiling. "Where are we supposed to get costumes the day before Christmas Eve? The closest thing I have to a Dickens-era gown is an old bridesmaid dress from my cousin's wedding, and I have no idea where it is."

"Oh, not to worry. Brenda will supply our wardrobe. She designs costumes for local theater companies. She's bringing a rack of dresses and suits in various sizes this afternoon."

"Wow." I imagined myself wearing a dress that was so huge I could barely get through the door. Come to think of it, I'd always wanted to wear a dress like that.

"You know what? This might be fun."

Lydia stood and went back to assessing the dining room. "I'm glad you think so."

A stalky woman from the housekeeping staff whizzed past us with a pushcart of linens and cleaning products. She swerved to avoid a life-sized nutcracker. I pictured her in an old fashion maid's outfit.

Brenda Murray. Why did I feel like I knew that name before taking her call yesterday?

Lydia pressed her fingertips to her forehead. "I gave too many people Christmas Eve off. What is wrong with me?"

I touched my boss's arm. There was no telling her that the Murrays could not expect so much on short notice. What a guest wanted a guest got if we could provide it. Lydia's tension told me that she definitely needed the snow globe in my bag.

"Relax, okay? At least she doesn't expect us to get our own costumes, hire carolers, or figure out how to serve roast goose,

plum pudding, and flaming rum punch. Our decorations will
work for the Dickens theme." I headed toward the Garden
Room at the back of the restaurant. I pointed to the Christmas
tree with its vintage ornaments and red balls. "See? It's perfect.
And the one in the lobby looks like it belongs in a magazine.
I'll just move the American Santa and the snowman to the back
room and anything else that looks too modern. You can switch
the music in the sound system to the Classical Christmas collec-
tion, and I'll see what other decorations we have for the tables."

"What if they plan to do party games that involve flying
objects."

"We'll figure it out."

She squeezed my hand. "You're amazing! And Brenda hired
her own carolers."

"Of course she did." Good thing we had a piano in the
Garden Room.

"Would it be at all possible for you to help serve the dinner
tomorrow, instead of working the front desk? It'll mean working
later."

"Are you kidding? I'm not missing out on something like
this!" Plus, I might get tips.

"Would you really?"

"I was a server at Applebee's in college. It'll bring back
memories." Once again, I got flooded with thoughts of Alex.
He'd come into Applebee's every Tuesday night with his study
group for biochemistry. That was how we met. He was premed
and always ordered the same thing: a patty melt with extra crispy
fries and a root beer, easy on the ice. He dipped his fries in bar-
becue sauce instead of ketchup.

Lydia reached out to hug me. "Thank you, *thank you*."

I patted her back. "No problem."

Lydia pulled away and took yet another deep breath. "I feel
better now." Then she held up a finger. "Wait, we need to figure

out one more thing. A place to hide Santa Claus. Excuse me, Father Christmas."

"I'm sure we can find a room."

At least with this dinner-to-remember, I wouldn't have time to entertain memories of Alex or overthink my decision to return Jason's present.

Chapter 4

I draped the forest green dress over my arm, so it wouldn't drag across the hallway floor on my way to the living room. "Aunt Sheila, can you please help?"

She put her hand over her heart as soon as she saw me. "Oh, Justine, hold up your dress so I can see the whole thing again." She blew her nose into a wad of cheap tissue.

I gripped the top of the dress and held it in front of me. Lydia had given me first pick of the costumes as a thank you for saving her Christmas Eve. I'd immediately claimed this green satin gown trimmed with cream colored lace. The hem was scalloped and reached all the way to the floor, so it would hide my twenty-first century black flats and tights. "How did women manage so many layers?"

"And you aren't even required to wear a corset."

"Shhh. Brenda Murray might hear you and bring a box of corsets tonight that she completely forgot yesterday." I carefully laid my gorgeous dress over the back of the sofa and pulled my long hair up in back. "I can't decide what to do with my hair."

My aunt sniffed and gave me the once over. "Sit down."

I took a place at the kitchen table. "Aunt Sheila, are you sick?" The last time Sheila got a bad cold it turned into pneumonia, and she spent New Year in the hospital. She was more upset about being stuck in a hospital bed than being dangerously ill. She was missing a New Year's Eve party.

"No, I just heard one of those Christmas songs." She swatted a tear with just enough flair to reflect how aware she was of her hypersensitivity to sentimental lyrics.

"Which song?" For years, it was the song about the boy trying to buy a pair of shoes for his dying mother for Christmas Eve. Then she couldn't get through the one with military families wishing each other Merry Christmas from across the globe.

She twisted my hair up in back and held it in place, "It was the song about peace on earth."

"Which one?"

She tried another style. "Does it really matter? They all wreck me."

They wrecked me too.

She let my hair flop over my shoulders. "Okay, I have an idea. Do you have any red satin ribbon?"

"I'm sure I do."

"You get that, and I'll get everything else."

By the time I returned from my craft stash with a spool of thin red ribbon and a long strand of gold, Sheila was coming down the hall with a curling iron, a brush, a mirror, hair spray, and a pink plastic accessory box that I remembered from when I used to play dress-up in her closet with my cousins.

My aunt plugged in the curling iron and handed me the accessory box. I opened it and found a selection of jeweled clips, bobby pins, and hair elastics.

"I feel like I'm getting ready for prom." Except I hadn't gone to prom. I didn't have a boyfriend at the time and couldn't afford a ticket or a spot on the party bus to go with friends. Going to a Christmas formal with Alex during sophomore year of college had made up for it. That formal was our first real date other than having coffee together. He'd whistled and whispered, "Wow," when he saw me in the burgundy dress I'd borrowed from my roommate.

Aunt Sheila set another box in front of me. "For you to borrow."

I opened it. Her wedding earrings. For as long as I could remember, she'd worn these pearl teardrops to every special event. "Are you sure?"

"Of course, I'm sure. They'll look perfect with that dress. Besides, you never know." She squeezed my shoulders and pressed her cheek against mine. "You might meet a fella?"

I smirked. A fella? "I'm pretty sure all the fellas will be too worried about keeping their top hats from falling into their dinner to notice me. I'm not looking for a fella anyway."

She picked up the curling iron and a small section of my hair. "Honey. It's time."

"You're a Happy Single Lady. Why not let me be one, too?"

"Because you're young and pretty and haven't had a date since your breakup with Alex. I, on the other hand, am more than twice your age, and have been on enough awkward dates in the fifteen years since my husband passed away to decide that I like being single."

"I thought you already had the perfect man picked out for me at church." Steven with the sweet hazel eyes.

She made another curl. "I do. But it's nice to have options."

"We don't even know Steven other than his first name and what he looks like. What if he's married."

"He's not. I asked one of the ushers."

"You're terrible."

For the next few minutes, we sat in silence while Sheila made curl after curl that would hopefully last the night. Then she broke the silence. "I promised myself I wouldn't pressure you, but have you given any more thought to Jason's package?"

Sweet quiet moment over. Thanks, Aunt Sheila. That package had kept me from sleeping half the night.

"Because if you changed your mind, I could wrap it, so it looks as nice as the ones I've seen you walk out the door with lately."

My heart wrenched. "I haven't changed my mind." I twisted a long piece of red ribbon around my fingers. "I'm dropping it off at the post office as soon as I get off work tonight. It's small enough for the drop box."

"Well, I think you're being silly. I'm not telling you to invite Jason to Christmas dinner, just accept his kindness and call him to say thank you. Text him even." She took the ribbon out of my hand and reached into a drawer for a pair of scissors. "It's one thing to have boundaries and another to be rude."

What could I possibly say to that? I opted for handing my aunt a sparkly clip for my hair. Before going to bed last night, a childish temptation to shake Jason's package had come over me. Jason had given the best gifts. He always knew exactly what Mom and I wanted. Even now, I wanted to know what he sent. But it was already in my tote bag with the last gift from my 12 Days of Christmas box, marked Return to Sender.

"I'm sure you already know this, but we're only torturing ourselves when we hold on to resentment." Aunt Sheila used her Sunday school teacher voice for emphasis.

"I know." I'd been feeling the torture since yesterday.

"Well then."

I turned around to face the aunt who took me in when I crushed my mother's heart by dropping out of college and breaking up with one of the few trustworthy guys that the McNally women had encountered in three generations. The aunt who believed I could do a lot more than manage the reservation desk of a hotel/restaurant that only still existed because it bore the label *historic* and provided the perfect setting for small weddings,

Jane Austen inspired teas, and, as of tonight, Charles Dickens theme parties. She did all of her over-the-top decorating for me knowing that as a kid I only got a loved-to-death artificial tree, dollar store Advent calendars filled with waxy chocolate, and cranberry candles from Mom's secret Santa at work. Her life had been just as rocky as mine and Mom's, yet she still cried over Christmas songs. No wonder I couldn't think of a good comeback.

She nudged me to turn around and used the clip I'd given her to secure a curl. "Justine, you are such a tenderhearted, generous, strong young woman. Don't ruin who you are by becoming bitter."

A sudden arrival of tears threatened to ruin my makeup. I forced them back. "Yesterday you mentioned Mom—that she has forgiven Jason, so why can't I? Well, Mom doesn't know the whole story."

"Maybe she knows more than you think. Besides, Jason is reaching out to you this time, not your mom."

I let the cinnamon and clove scented air calm my cluttered mind. I couldn't decide what scared me more, the idea of becoming bitter or forgiving Jason and getting burned again. I also didn't want to be a person who could be bought with a trinket.

"I know it's time to let go of what he did, Aunt Sheila. I'm just not ready to accept presents from him yet."

She reached for another clip and sighed. "I guess I can understand that. But you might want to reconsider doing a Return to Sender without explanation."

I nodded. It did seem cold the more I thought about it. I could include a note.

After many more curls and clips, some twisting, and several strands of ribbon, my aunt handed me a dish towel to hold in front of my face while she sprayed her creation. "Tell you what.

I don't want to spoil your night or your Christmas. So I promise not to bring it up again."

"Thank you," I said through the dish towel.

"Do you want to see your hair?"

"Yes, please." I set the towel on the table and picked up the mirror.

My hair was a gloriously outdated mass of fat curls twisted back with the jeweled clips and ribbons. A stream of red and gold ribbon strands hung down the back.

"You look so pretty, Justine."

I smiled at my reflection and added the earrings. "I love it." I could hardly speak. It was like playing dress-up again, but so much better.

My aunt tugged on the silver half-heart pendant I'd received so long ago. "Don't forget to take that off."

"I'll put it in my makeup bag when I change at work." I stood up and hugged her. "Thank you so much."

"You are so welcome."

"Love you."

"Love you, too." She patted my arms. "See you at church later?"

Church would definitely be a good thing. I gathered my armload and headed to the door. "I'm supposed to get off at nine, but I have no idea how long this spectacle will last. I'll most likely be late. Since you'll be with the choir, I'll find a seat on my own and meet you afterward."

"Sounds like a plan."

"Merry Christmas, Aunt Sheila." I swung the door open, careful not to knock the wreath from its hanger with my dress. The outdoor twinkle lights performed their Merry Christmas dance in the late afternoon haze.

"Have Lydia take a picture of you."

"I'm sure there will be lots of pictures." As if we would need pictures to remember this night.

The twirly bow from Gift #12 poked out of my tote bag and brushed against my arm. How would I feel if I handed this present to someone, and they shoved it right back in my face?

Maybe I should give the *Grace* cross to my aunt. She seemed to have a much better grasp on grace than I did.

Chapter 5

Usually I would be bummed out about working on Christmas Eve, but today I was thankful for the distraction from my personal Ghosts of Christmas Past.

There were times when I felt like an unreasonable brat for holding onto my grudge against Jason, and this was definitely one of those times. I knew girls who had far worse complaints than mine—true horror stories. Jason, who once felt more like a real father than the man whose name appeared on my birth certificate, had never laid an unloving or inappropriate hand on me. Unlike the many boyfriends who came between Mom's first marriage and him, Jason was a faithful, unaddicted Christ follower with a good job. But losing that good job and attempting to start his own car repair business, only to have it fail, put him in debt up to his hair follicles. As Mom and I learned, desperation can push a person to do unbelievable things.

It stung enough when he slowly drained the bank account intended for my college expenses not covered by financial aid and scholarships. He had already depleted his and Mom's savings, so I knew it would be a while before he replaced my money as promised. Then Mom's mother died and left her a set of one hundred-year-old wedding china. Grandma left me a ruby bracelet that had belonged to her mother. The diamonds accenting the six small rubies were miniscule, but I would've treasured it even if the stones were fake. I didn't know my ancestors had anything that nice. And grandma had left it to *me*.

I tried to focus on driving, but my mind kept drifting. This time to the three-day weekend when I was home from college and Jason asked to see my bracelet. It was something I only wore on special occasions, and Alex was taking me out for a nice dinner to celebrate his getting into medical school. After admiring it, Jason said, "I suggested to your mom that we get the china appraised for insurance purposes. How about if I take your bracelet in, too?"

I'd always wondered how much a bracelet like that was worth, so the next day I gave it to him without hesitation or feeling the need to mention it to Mom. After all, it was my bracelet, and she probably knew he planned to take it.

Mom called two weeks later, crying so hard that I could barely understand her.

"Jason sold my mother's china to an antique dealer. We didn't even discuss it. He said he was getting it appraised, not planning to sell it. This explains the lame excuses he gave me when I asked why the appraiser was taking so long for something as simple as china." It had been worth more than Mom expected, which must have been why Jason decided they needed the money more than antique plates and serving dishes.

I kept waiting for her to mention my bracelet. That was when it hit me that she didn't know Jason had asked me for it. Mom was so devastated by the betrayal that I didn't mention it. Instead I confronted Jason myself.

"I'm so sorry, Justine," was all he could manage. It was his answer to all of my tearful questions. I'm sorry.

I could hear in his voice how sorry he was. But it wasn't enough.

Mom left Jason, not because of the money or the china but because she could no longer trust him. I cried with Alex over the same thing then started pulling away from him. If Jason could turn out to be a lying thief, how could I expect Alex to be any different. Clearly the McNally women attracted creeps, and the best way to break the cycle was to stay away from guys.

Fast-forward a decade and, as of two weeks ago, Jason was back in Mom's life "as a friend for now," supposedly a different person who "has never been able to forgive himself for stealing from us."

Good. He should feel guilty. Forever.

But how much longer did I expect to avoid him? What if Mom invited him over for Christmas? Aunt Sheila and I were hosting this year, but she could still show up with him. By then, his gift would be in the mail.

Chapter 6

*L*ydia tied a fat bow around an old-time lamp that she'd found in the storage room. She stepped back. "What do you think? Is the bow too much?"

I fingered my heart pendant, pulling it back and forth on its chain. "No, I think it's cute."

We found a corner opposite the Christmas tree to plug it in and surrounded it with some leftover snow fabric from the villages in the lobby.

The Garden Room didn't look exactly like a page out of Dickens, but with the help of a candelabra that I found in the back room and decorated with greenery, a lamp post, and dim lighting it came pretty close. We'd set up two long tables for Brenda Murray's family and a round one by the piano for the carolers. Once people started arriving, we would turn on the fireplace.

The Dickens theme brought me back to the first Christmas with Jason, when he took me and Mom to San Francisco to see the musical *Scrooge*. I was twelve and, other than an abridged version of *The Nutcracker* in the fourth grade, I had never seen a major stage production. Before the show he took us to have clam chowder at Boudin and to see the giant Christmas tree at Union Square. We watched the ice skaters, and he said we'd put skating on the list for next year. He was the first man in Mom's life to keep a promise like that.

Why this flood of memories when I had a job to do?

Lydia checked her watch. "We better get dressed lest Brenda Murray should catch us out of uniform."

I laughed and wrapped my arm around her as we walked to the women's restroom to change clothes. "I wonder what happens to people who are guilty of such a crime."

"I don't know, but I'm sure it's extremely painful."

Lydia and I took turns in the largest stall. I let her go first and touched up my makeup. I could hear her wrestling with the royal blue gown she'd selected and was about to offer help when she called my name through the stall door.

"Justine, I found the most precious thing after you went home last night."

I smiled, knowing what she'd found. "What was it?"

Lydia came out holding up the hem of her dress. "I found a present with my name on it, beside my computer. It was a snow globe with the cutest snow people inside, and a handful of peppermint candy. The snow globe makes me smile every time I look at it. I put the candy in a fancy dish for tomorrow."

"Who was it from?"

"I don't know. It included a card with a Bible verse—the one about the God of hope filling you with joy and peace—but no signature." She turned around. "Could you zip me, please?"

I found the zipper and pulled it up, thankful that our costumes weren't so old fashioned that I had to secure a long row of buttons. "Maybe you have a secret admirer."

"My husband might have something to say about that." She reached for a hat decorated with bows and lace to cover her short hair.

"True." I took my dress into the stall.

"I wish I knew who left it, so I could thank them. I put the snow globe on my nightstand, so I can see it first thing every morning."

"My aunt told me once that people who leave anonymous gifts don't want to be thanked. The joy of giving in secret is their blessing." She told me this when I received my 12 Days of Christmas box and wished I could thank the person who sent it.

"That is a remarkable thought." She knocked on the stall door. "How you doing in there?"

I took the first step into my dress. "Good. But I'm sure I'll need a zip-up."

Once I had my dress all the way up and had slipped into my flats, I let my boss zip the back then did a little twirl like when I was five.

As soon as I was facing her, Lydia cocked her head to one side and grinned. "Aw, you look just like a Christmas doll that I had as a little girl."

I fluff out the front of my dress. "Oh, stop." Christmas doll was not the look I'd been going for.

"It's a compliment, sweetie. That was my all-time favorite doll." She looked into my eyes. "It's my creative way of saying you look beautiful. Especially your hair."

I blushed. "Thank you. My aunt did it." I ran my hands over the green satin skirt. "I love this shade of green."

"And it loves you." She adjusted her hat. "So, you ready to make this party happen?"

I grabbed my makeup bag and the clothes I'd arrived in. "Yes. Let's go see how many Christmas ghosts we can fit at one table."

The jingle bells on the entrance door tinkled. A striking middle-aged woman in a red Dickens-era ball gown rushed through the hotel's double doors clutching the hands of twin Tiny Tims. Her smile masked frantic eyes, a look that only one who'd been trained to impress could manage. This had to be Brenda Murray. I'd been on my break when she dropped off the costumes yesterday and missed meeting her in person. I took my place behind the reservation desk in case the young man and woman following her were some of the relatives needing a room. The couple's working-class garb gave away their roles as Bob Cratchit and wife.

I felt something cold against my neck. *Oh no. I slapped my hand over my necklace.* After discovering that my dress didn't have a single pocket, I tucked the pendant into my bodice, which was, thankfully, just high enough to hide it. I swooped curls and ribbon over my shoulders to cover the silver chain.

Mrs. Cratchit took the boys from the older woman and walked them past the reservation desk to the Christmas tree. She looked familiar. *That smile. I know those rosy cheeks and big brown eyes.*

My stomach did a cartwheel. I felt a sudden desire to hide under the desk but slapped on a welcoming smile instead. "Merry Christmas. May I help you?"

"Yes," the woman in the ball gown answered from across the room. "We're the Murray Party. The first part of it anyway. I'm Brenda."

"I'm Justine, Lydia's assistant manager and one of your hosts this evening."

Mrs. Cratchit knelt in front of the twins, her back to me. She adjusted their costumes and whispered a gentle warning about not using their pretend crutches as swords.

That younger-than-her-years voice. No one else on the planet had that voice.

It can't be her. It would be too weird.

"You do have our suite reservations. Please say I don't need to deal with another disaster."

The word *disaster* woke me up. "Um, yes." I prayed for my voice to stop quivering as I pulled up the reservation. "Your guests can check into their suites any time, and the Garden Room is all ready for you."

"Thank you so much. You saved our Christmas." She walked up behind the younger woman and touched her shoulder then pointed toward the Garden Room. "Amy, how about if you let Kevin take those crutches for now and put them in the Garden Room."

Amy. It is her.

Tiny Tim 1 and Tiny Tim 2 handed their crutches to Bob Cratchit who promised to give them back at the party.

The details rushed back to me. In college Alex's sister Amy dated a guy named Kevin Murray. He went to a different college, so I only saw him a few times, but they were already talking about marriage. Once, Alex and I went on a double date with Amy and Kevin, and Kevin's mom called with details about a family get-together. I could still see Amy leaning into her boyfriend's phone and greeting his mom with, "Hi, Brenda."

The twins had Amy's eyes.

God, no, please. I could not spend Christmas Eve serving my ex-boyfriend's sister.

Chapter 7

Watching Lydia transform her tense face into a smile and greet Brenda Murray reminded me that I had volunteered to do exactly that—serve the sister of someone I'd treated terribly.

I wished for a fever, a violent onslaught of food poisoning, anything to get out of this party. Maybe Aunt Sheila really had been sick when she styled my hair, and I caught her cold. I cleared my throat and coughed into my arm. I swallowed, hoping to feel pain in my throat. Nothing. I was annoyingly healthy.

Amy followed her husband and Brenda to the Garden Room without giving me as much as a glance. *Thank you, God.* Soon the whole Murray clan would be here, forcing me to follow through on my promise to play nineteenth-century waitress.

This must be my punishment for refusing Jason's gift.

I knew Lydia needed me to do more than stand paralyzed in the server station. The Cratchits, Scrooge, Jacob Marley, all three Christmas ghosts, and an array of beautifully dressed party guests had just ordered drinks and appetizers. They'd just finished a game of Yes and No, which to Lydia's relief, only involved each person choosing an animal name out of a hat. A harp duet plucked out "God Rest Ye Merry Gentlemen" over the sound system. *Let nothing you dismay . . .*

Really?

Yasmin, our newest server, grabbed a tray of water and looked at me with *Are you going to help, or what?* written all over her face.

Lydia flew past the little nook. She stopped and poked her head in. "Justine." She did not sound happy. "Does your offer to help me still stand?"

I grabbed a glass and filled it with ice. "Coming, sorry."

She stepped into the server station, her dress rustling. "What is going on with you all of a sudden? Yasmin is doing literally everything while you hang out in here."

The glass in my hand felt like a giant weight. My mind spun. She needed an answer.

"Are you okay?"

I set the glass down and did a thumb thrust over my shoulder. My words sounded silly before I got them out. "My ex-boyfriend's sister is in there."

"And?"

"And." And what? "It's really awkward."

Lydia's eyes told me how quickly I'd gone from amazing and beautiful to immature. She reached for a tray and set it down in front of me. "Listen, I don't mean to minimize your angst, but for tonight that woman is a customer, okay? If she is rude to you, be polite and let it go as you would for anyone else. If you need to fall apart later, I'll be right here." She smacked my back. "You can do this."

I sucked in my breath and blew out slowly. "Okay."

The Amy I knew in college didn't have it in her to be openly rude, and as far as I could tell, she hadn't changed a bit. At the very worst she would ignore me or send pitiful glances my way. After all, Alex probably had a gorgeous wife and at least one child by now. I filled the glass with water, set it on the tray, filled three more, pasted on a smile, and forced my feet into the dining room.

Too bad my weight or hair color hadn't changed since college, making me utterly unrecognizable. I dodged one of the Tiny Tims on my way to the table. The other one sat beside Amy, dipping his straw into his water glass, holding it up, and watching drips hit the table. She took the straw and moved the glass out of reach then reached out for the other twin. Those across from her were the ones in need of water. She would know me in two seconds, even with the fancy dress and curls. She remembered everyone.

I avoided making eye contact by positioning myself sideways, but Jacob Marley's chain almost tripped me. I steadied myself before dropping the whole tray of water into his lap. I set one water glass down then another. Again, Amy had to tell one of her boys to stop playing with his water. She reminded them about restaurant manners.

Good, she's too busy to notice me. Please boys, keep the bad table manners going as long as you want.

I set the last glass down and made my escape.

Back in the server station, I let the empty tray fall on the counter and leaned my head back, releasing my relief. *I did it.* Then I heard it; the does-anything-ever-get-her-down voice from a decade ago. She was right behind me.

"Justine? I thought that was you."

Breathe. In. Out. Good girl. Did she sound mad? Not at all. I gathered the courage to turn. She didn't look mad either.

"Amy?" I said it as if I'd just made the connection.

"I almost didn't recognize you in that dress, but then I realized, oh my gosh, it's Justine McNally."

I waited for her face to contort into a glare. Instead, the smile I remembered spread across Amy's joyful face. She picked up her skirt and rushed over to me, right there in the server station. She threw her arms around my neck, pulling me into one of her perfect hugs. "How are you?"

"Good." *Liar.* Her hug dissolved the years. We might as well have been back in the student union grabbing lunch between classes.

She squeezed my hands. "I can't believe this."

Believe me, neither can I.

"You look great." She backed up. "And you got my favorite gown. It's perfect on you."

That's my cue to say something.

Strands of straight dark hair had escaped Amy's bun. The tiny frame I remembered had filled out, but she had also carried twins. Even in a poor woman's costume with hair that refused to behave, she looked as adorable as ever.

"You look great too."

She smoothed her skirt. "Aren't these outfits fun? My mother-in-law made them all. Designing period costumes is Brenda's retirement hobby. These are from a production of *A Christmas Carol* that she helped out with last year."

Yes, let's talk costumes. Anything to avoid the elephant. "They're incredible. I feel like I got sucked into a movie."

A very strange one.

"Me too." She lowered her voice to a whisper, "I won't pretend, I thought this idea was a bit extravagant, but now that we're here, it's so much fun."

"Brenda really knows how to throw a party."

"She does." Amy rested one hand on her tummy. "I'm just glad she made it alcohol free for the sake of the kids and the cost. I mean, can you imagine what this scene could turn into with costumes, canes, *and* cocktails?"

I hadn't even considered that. "Your mother-in-law is a wise woman."

"I know Brenda can be a little demanding, but she has a good heart. She adores the boys."

I tried to imagine Brenda Murray playing with kids.

"So, how long have you been working here?"

I got the job two weeks after moving in with Aunt Sheila. She knew Lydia through book club. I didn't feel ready to be out in public as the loser who dropped out of college, but Sheila insisted I needed the distraction. I wasn't about to confess any of that to Amy.

"Oh, for a while. What are you up to?" Surely, she was doing something far greater than working in a hotel. She'd majored in interior design.

The twins ran over and hugged her legs. She wrapped one arm around each of them. "Mostly chasing after these guys."

The boys looked up at me with their dancing brown eyes. I grabbed a glass and filled it with diet cola, completely forgetting the ice. "They're adorable. How old are you, boys?"

One of them held up three fingers and the other said, "Thwee."

"Four in February. Peter is wearing the red cap and James is in the green." She rubbed each of their heads. "Boys, say hello to Miss Justine."

They greeted me in stereo then she released them to go back to the table.

Amy let her gray shawl fall open and patted her stomach. "We're expecting again. Only one this time. A girl. We just found out."

"Congratulations." I pictured a baby girl that looked like a miniature version of Amy. Then I caught myself picturing what Alex's kids might look like.

Amy looked over her shoulder then back at me. "Oh, I wish you weren't working. I'd invite you to join us for dinner."

Had she suffered a terrible accident and forgotten what I did? I sneaked a glance at the table scene—the matching almost-four-year-old boys who were in the process of removing their caps, girls in ringlets, women in big dresses, people laughing and attempting to act like their characters, a cluster of teenagers whose faces revealed how they felt about Grandma's Christmas Eve costume party. If I hadn't freaked out, Alex would have asked me to marry him. The signs were all there. I could have been Amy's sister-in-law. Those cute little boys would be calling me Aunt Justine instead of Miss Justine.

I set the soda aside. "Well, maybe we can chat after the party." It would be past the boys' bedtime by then for sure, so she would most likely need to leave before that.

"Yes, let's do that. And find every excuse you can to come to the table, so I get to see you."

Before I could say, "Okay," Lydia waved me over. Amy gave me another grin and returned to her place beside Kevin Murray, who scratched at his high collar.

Lydia pulled me aside. "Everything okay?"

I nodded, sneaking a glance at Amy tying napkins around her boys' necks so they wouldn't mess up their suits. "Fine."

"Good. Can you find the light for the piano? The carolers are due to arrive any minute."

"Please say you don't need an accompanist, because I don't play."

"No, Brenda plays. And just as a heads up, when the carolers invite the family to join in the singing, the staff is welcome to sing along. She provided song sheets, so I'm guessing *welcome* means *required*."

I tried not to laugh. This just kept getting better.

"Be happy that it's just Christmas carols. Originally she wanted to reenact Fezziwig's ball."

By the time we served dinner, I had accepted the Garden Room as my home for the evening and Amy as a guest who no longer needed to be feared. I'd learned how to balance a tray while walking in a floor-length dress and dodging props.

"Mom," Amy said to Brenda after thanking me for her turkey dinner, "this is Justine, a friend from college."

I balanced my tray and smiled at Amy then at Brenda. "Small world, huh?"

She smiled back. "Very small. What a nice coincidence." She actually looked happy.

When I was taking dessert orders—pumpkin pie or peppermint ice cream—Amy introduced me to the Ghost of Christmas Past/Brenda's sister Loretta, again as her friend.

Breaking up with Alex had doubled as cutting Amy off. It had deeply hurt her feelings. She'd told me so in an email. *I don't understand why we can't still be friends.* Some friend I was.

A lump started forming in my throat. I managed to get out, "Nice to meet you" as Loretta tried to shake my hand and adjust her slipping white wig at the same time.

I was writing down that Amy wanted pumpkin pie when her boys shot up in their chairs.

A jolly male voice boomed from the Garden Room doorway, "Happy Christmas, one and all!" in a bad British accent. Every head in the room turned to see the figure in a majestic, flowing gold-and-white-trimmed red robe and long white beard. In his arms he cradled a gigantic red bag.

"Santa!" Peter shouted.

"No, remember?" Brenda corrected. "That's Father Christmas."

Brenda directed every child and teenager in the room to find a place on the bright red rug in front of the fireplace. Lydia moved a big chair in front of the children and directed Father Christmas to take a seat. Amy settled her boys into their spots and went back to her place. Kevin whispered something in her ear. For the first time that night, I saw Amy look like she was forcing a smile. She whispered something back to him. My next job was to help Yasmin serve dessert, so I started making my way to the server station. I looked over my shoulder at the kids and saw Amy talking to Lydia, then she started following me.

I wiped a blob of something sticky off my fingers and spotted Amy. "Can I get you something?"

She shook her head. "Lydia said you could take a break. She'll help Yasmin with dessert."

This seemed like an odd time for a break. "Okay."

Amy pulled me into an empty corner of the main part of the restaurant, worry shadowing her face. "I could probably get away with not telling you this, but it wouldn't be fair." She looked out of the corner of her eye at the scene in the Garden Room and whispered, "Alex is here."

Chapter 8

My knees almost gave out. "What?"

"Justine, I promise you, I had no idea."

Even in the corner that Amy had found for us, I had a clear view of the party. Father Christmas took a present out of his bag and called a little girl in a green plaid dress over. I instinctively backed up, looking around for the man I still couldn't get out of my mind. When had he sneaked in? "Where is he?"

Amy pointed toward the happy group by the fireplace. Father Christmas handed the little girl a box wrapped in candy cane-striped paper. He patted the little girl's head and called for the next child, forgetting to use the accent. A chill shot through my heart.

"A man that my brother-in-law works with was supposed to play Father Christmas, but he caught the flu from one of his grandkids. Brenda asked Alex last night. Kevin just told me."

My eyes remained frozen on the man by the fireplace, picturing the face I once loved underneath that long snowy beard. "Is his family here somewhere?"

Amy shook her head.

Good thing. Seeing his wife would put me over the edge. "Oh, of course not. His kids might recognize him and give him away."

Amy looked toward the gift-giving scene. "Alex isn't married."

Something in my cried out, *He's free!*

What was I thinking? Free? I'd probably ruined his ability to have a decent relationship. I fumbled for words, any words. "That's too bad. He would make a nice husband and a great dad."

"Yes, he would." Amy folded her arms and watched Father Christmas reach into his sack. "Too bad he never got the chance to be one."

The lump rose in my throat again as I watched the nicest guy in the world pat Peter on the head and send him away with a small rectangular box.

She looked at my face. "I'm sorry. That came out all wrong. He just never found the right person."

"No, I'm fine. It's just…" A sigh came out way more dramatically than intended. I wished for a chair to sink into. "I was so stupid."

Amy elbowed me. "Yes, you were." She leaned against the doorframe and watched her son tear the wrapping paper off his package. "Hey, Justine, maybe this is none of my business, but I think Alex being my brother gives me special privileges."

I prepared myself for what I knew was coming.

"Why did you dump my brother?"

Dump. Now that I didn't expect. That ugly word drove home what I'd done—tossed a wonderful man aside like junk.

"He really loved you."

I looked around for Lydia. How long of a break had she approved? "I know he did. I loved him too."

"You were perfect for each other."

We were. Our backgrounds couldn't have been more different, but in every other area we fit like a puzzle.

"It's like one day you two were making us all sick with how cute you were, and the next you needed space. It didn't make sense."

No, it didn't. Ten years later it made absolutely no sense at all. I spilled out my only defense.

"Did Alex tell you what my stepfather did?"

"That he stole some things from you and your mom? Yes, he told me." Amy stepped back from the doorway and looked at me with moist eyes. "I can't even image how that must have felt."

Father Christmas's toy bag got in the way of his robe, pushing it back and revealing a pair of tennis shoes. At least the stripes matched his robe.

"That's why I broke up with Alex."

"And what your stepdad did was Alex's fault because?"

Reality, along with the shift in Amy's tone, hit me like a punch in the stomach. Of course it wasn't Alex's fault. The need to be understood shoved aside the onslaught of remorse. "Jason—my stepdad—was the first man that really took care of me and my mom. My dad never came around, and before Jason, every relationship that Mom had turned into a nightmare. She used to joke that collecting losers was a family tradition."

Amy let out a laugh but looked at me like she felt sorry for doing it.

"Jason did everything I imagined a dad would do. He helped me with my homework, took us to church, came to my soccer games, got teary when he saw me in my high school graduation gown. Then he started having financial problems." I told her the rest.

Instead of an outpouring of sympathy, Amy said, "I still don't understand what that had to do with Alex."

I watched Father Christmas give James a big hug and lift him up off his feet. My lip trembled. "I didn't want to wait around for Alex to fail me, too."

He expression softened again. "Alex is just as capable of failing you as anyone. Face it, we humans are masters at letting each other down. But he would never hurt you on purpose."

No, he wouldn't.

"Alex thought you were the one God had in mind for him."

"I thought the same thing." Tears started to trickle before I had a chance to feel them coming. I turned my back to the party scene. "He must hate me."

She shook her head. "He never hated you." She adjusted the shawl around her shoulders. "Okay, I confess, Alex was crushed. He never expected you to treat him like that, and frankly, neither did I. I felt ditched, too. You were like a sister to me. One day a lady at church saw me crying and I told her what happened. She encouraged me to pray for you. At first, I was like, what? Are you kidding me? I was looking for sympathy, lady, not a sermon. Later, I decided okay, fine, I'm tired of being mad, I'll try it. It helped a lot. But it took a long time for losing your friendship to stop hurting. It took a lot longer for Alex."

My tears trickled faster, my body shaking as I fought against sobs. "Amy, I am so sorry."

Amy stroked my arm. "I forgive you. And I know Alex would say the same thing." Then she gave me a tender took and held out her arms. "Oh, come here. Please don't cry so much. It's Christmas!" She wrapped me in another tight hug. "Justine, my timing can be so bad sometimes. I shouldn't have brought this up tonight."

The fact that I needed to get back to work forced me to pull myself together. "No, I'm glad we talked about it."

"The whole family forgives you."

"Thank you," I choked out.

She rubbed my back and gently pulled away. She patted her pockets. "I can't believe that with two preschoolers I don't have tissue."

I swept my fingers across my cheeks and under my eyes and sniffed hard. "Modern tissue wouldn't go with your outfit."

"A handkerchief then." She squeezed my shoulder. The thunder of pint-sized feet brought our moment to an abrupt halt.

"Mommy! Look what Fathur Santa gave me."

I turned to hide my tears from Peter as he held out a small old-fashioned train.

"Wow." Amy knelt in front of Peter and admired the train. "It's the one you wanted."

"Open it, please."

"Let's wait until we get home in case it has parts that might get lost."

James sneaked up from behind and thrust a toy sports car in front of Amy's face. "I got this."

Amy popped her head back in surprise. "Whoa, that is so cool."

She was the best mom I'd ever seen in action, clearly in love with her kids. I even found it a little refreshing to know her boys weren't above using their straws as drip toys.

James leaned on Amy's shoulder and rubbed his eyes. He stroked her neck, taking hold of something under her collar.

"No, no, James. That needs to stay hidden." She looked up at me. "I forgot to take off my necklace. Brenda made me tuck it in because it's not authentic."

I pulled up my necklace with my index fingers. "Guilty. You did a much better job of hiding yours."

James pointed to my necklace. "That's *Mommy's* broken heart."

Amy's face reddened a little. "That's right. It does look like Mommy's." She kissed her little boy's cheek. "Leave your toys here and go see what your cousins got."

Mommy's broken heart? I focused in on the silver chain still poking out of the top of Amy's costume.

The boys took off. Amy propped their gifts against the wall. I wrapped my fingers around the half-heart dangling against my dress.

"Amy, can I see your necklace?" I stroked the praying hands on my pendant. "Please?"

Amy's eyes protested but only for a moment. She took a step closer and pulled the necklace out of her collar. At the end of the chain hung a silver half-heart. Mine had cracks on the left, hers had cracks on the right. The part of me that had watched way too many Hallmark movies with Aunt Sheila wanted to press my half against hers, forming a perfect fit. Instead I stated the obvious. "You sent me the Christmas box."

"Yes." She faked a pout and stomped her foot. "It was supposed to stay a secret forever." Amy threw up her arms up. "Oh, well, secret's out. Thanks a lot, James."

Tears almost started up again. "I can't believe you did that after how I treated your brother. And you."

"I couldn't either at the time, to be honest. But I guess that's what happens when you try praying for someone that you're mad at. I figured you had to be going through something major to leave Alex."

More like temporary insanity.

"But the handwriting on the cards." I would have known Amy's loopy cursive. "It wasn't like yours at all."

"I paid my roommate a dollar per card to write them out for me."

Between the gifts and paying her roommate, she must have spent a small fortune on me.

I wiped under my eyes again, dreading what I must look like, overcome with the desire to tell her what her generosity inspired. But we didn't have time. "Amy, that box of presents meant so much to me. I didn't just dump a great guy. I let a sweet friend go, too."

She draped her arm around me and squeezed. "We make crazy choices when we're hurt and scared. Your stepdad did something he probably regrets now. And so did you. When I get a chance to fill you in on the last ten years, you'll find out that I've had my share of regrettable moments. Trust me. That's why we need forgiveness and grace, from God and from each other."

Father Christmas set aside his empty red sack and pulled a bundle of candy canes from the pocket of his robe.

"I will never stop being sorry."

Amy winked. "He's still single, remember?"

"Oh, come on, what am I going to do? Ask to get back together?"

"You should probably start with, 'I'm sorry.'"

"Yeah, probably."

For a moment we both just stood there, watching one kid after another, including the teenagers, hug Father Christmas, get their picture taken, and run off with a candy cane.

Amy leaned her head toward mine. "Alex was such a good sport to agree to hide in his dressing room until the party ends."

Father Christmas shouted a final Happy Christmas. Brenda took her place at the piano and called the carolers up for another song. How would I ever keep my mind on work with Alex in the building? "I'll have some food sent to him."

Amy picked up her kids' toys. "Brenda told him not to show his face in the lobby until at least nine o'clock, and he must be out of costume." She gave me another quick hug. "I better relieve Kevin and let you get back to work. Don't let me leave without getting your email address and phone number, so we can get together."

"I look forward to hearing about your regrettable choices."

She laughed. Then she stopped at the door to the Garden Room. "And regarding the bit of information I just gave you? I don't really need to say, 'Hint, hint' do I?"

Chapter 9

Amy waved to me while ushering her sleepy boys out the door. I waved back, sneaking another glance at the grandfather clock. It was nine o'clock exactly. The overnight guests were slowly making their way upstairs.

Brenda Murray stopped at the reservation desk holding the twins' toys. She handed Lydia two envelopes. "I know we already left a tip for the dinner, but this is a little something extra for you and Justine."

Lydia accepted the envelope and thanked her. "I'm happy that we could make this happen for you, Brenda. I enjoyed watching your family have such a good time."

"It was a great party," I assured her. "I can't believe you made all these clothes."

She appeared to be blushing. "Oh, it's just a little hobby of mine." Brenda set the toys down on the counter. "I want to tell you both how much I appreciate all of your hard work. I know I asked a lot of you on short notice, and if I came across as one of those nightmare customers, I apologize. Oh, let's face it. I know I did. But I will be recommending this place often, so I hope the added business makes up for my behavior."

Lydia put her hands over Brenda's. "If my house had flooded the day before guests were due to arrive and Santa got sick on top of that, my behavior would've made yours look understated."

I raised my hand. "Mine would've been worse than Lydia's. I have a story from yesterday as proof."

Lydia shot me a took. "Oh, really?"

"Just trust me."

Brenda laughed out loud and wished us both Merry Christmas. "I'll pick the costumes up after New Year." She started toward the door then stopped. "I've been staying with Kevin and Amy since the flood, so Christmas morning should be quite an adventure with the boys."

Her smile told me she was looking forward to it.

As soon as Brenda left, Lydia took off her hat and ran her fingers through her hair. "Now to get out of this dress."

"You must admit this went better than expected."

"It did. And you were right. It *was* fun. Even in these crazy getups." She came over and gave me a big hug. "I could not have done it without you."

"I'm glad I could help." I forced myself to look at her instead of at the clock.

"And I take it everything went okay with your ex-boy-friend's sister. I saw you having a pretty tender discussion with Brenda's daughter-in-law. Was that her?"

"That was her." I watched the stairs and the elevator door. "It went better than okay."

"I want to hear the whole saga after Christmas." She picked up her hat. "For now, I am going home and to bed. The night staff just started showing up, so you're free to go." She handed me my envelope then reached for my hand and gave it a squeeze. "Merry Christmas, sweet girl."

"Merry Christmas."

The elevator door opened right after Lydia left the lobby.

I had been expecting him, but my heart still jumped when I saw Alex exit the elevator with a garment bag slung over his arm and a backpack over his shoulder. The absence of his false beard revealing a more distinguished version of the face I knew. His dark hair had receded a tiny bit. He rubbed his chin, peeling off remaining flecks of adhesive.

I stood frozen beside the reservation desk, rebuking the voice in my head telling me to forget the whole encounter and run off to change before he saw me. *No, this is my only chance.*

"Alex?" I sounded like an eight-year-old.

He looked my way, stopping by the giant nutcracker. I pushed away my unrealistic desire to have him rush over and envelop me in his arms, carrying on about how long he'd dreamed of this night.

"Justine. Hi." He stayed put. "Amy told me you were here. I saw you earlier."

"You had a job to do."

He rubbed his face again. "Yeah."

"You make a great Father Christmas."

He chuckled. "Thanks. I would only make such an idiot out of myself for James and Peter." He waved his hand toward me. "I see you didn't get out of the costume thing either."

I reached up and touched my hair. My curls had started to droop. "No. But it was worth it."

We exchanged awkward acknowledgements of how great each other looked. Then silence opened the door for what I needed to get out. I willed my feet to move his way and my voice to work properly. "Alex, before we get caught up in so-what-have-you-been-up-to-since-college small talk, I need to say something."

He laid his costume over a chair and his backpack beside it. "Okay."

"I am truly sorry for hurting you." I'd planned to pour out my reasons again but covering an apology with excuses didn't feel right anymore. "What I did... You didn't deserve it."

His lips turned up at the corners. His eyes smiled. "I forgive you. I forgave you a long time ago."

I wanted so badly to bury my face against his chest. Instead I looked into his gentle eyes. "Thank you."

"I know what happened with Jason really affected you."

"It did, but I should have trusted you." I was about to cry again. "You never gave me a reason not to."

"Justine." He reached out and squeezed my hand. "You're forgiven."

All I could do was nod.

He let go of my hand much too quickly and sat on the edge of one of the couches. "Things are good for you now?"

As long as this lasts, things are perfect. "Yes, much better."

He smiled. "Good."

The question of what to say after that brought us back to the small talk. Before we knew it, we were catching up without the uncomfortable distance. He was a pediatrician, right here in town, just like he'd always wanted to be, leaving me feeling like an underachiever. He and Amy and everyone else I knew had moved forward while I stayed stuck, held prisoner by resentment.

"So, how is your aunt that you always talked about?"

"Sheila. She's great. We share an apartment." She would be crazy with joy right now. *That's right, Aunt Sheila!* I looked at the clock again. "I'm supposed to meet her at church in, um, half an hour ago."

Alex picked up his garment bag. "I should let you get going."

No, please don't let me get going. She'll be thrilled if a say I skipped church for a guy.

"It was great seeing you." He turned toward the door.

I called out to him before he could get away.

He looked over his shoulder in the way that always made me melt. "Yeah?"

"Would you like to ..." I swallowed the *start over* trying to fly out of my mouth. "... get coffee or something. Not now, obviously. But after the holidays?"

He brushed something off his garment bag then looked back at me. "That would be nice."

"I know a great coffee place near here."

"Full 'a Beans?"

"How did you know?"

"I always thought it seems like a place you would like."

Chapter 10

I hurried to my car, dying to squeal, "I have a date with Alex the day after New Year!" even though it wasn't exactly a date, just coffee. Jason's present sat abandoned on the passenger seat, covered with a sweatshirt. The sight of it snuffed out the thrill of a second chance.

Why did I suddenly feel like Jason and I had a lot in common?

I hadn't stolen anything. But I had hurt two people deeply. One of them prayed for me and sent me presents. The one I wounded the most forgave me long before I asked him to.

Your stepdad did something he probably regrets now.

The package sitting beside me and an ignored text message cried out that he did.

I picked up the package and set it in my lap, moisture once again stinging my eyelids. I pulled at the packing tape.

Not yet.

I dug my phone out of my tote bag and pulled up Jason's text. My fingers shook so badly that I had to delete three mistakes before finally entering *I got it. I just haven't opened it yet. Thank you.* I hit Send.

I wiped the last of my tears and slipped the phone back into my bag. Red curling ribbon shimmered under the streetlights. *My gift.* In all the drama of today I'd never given it away. I should've given it to Amy. Or Brenda. Or…

It took twenty-five minutes to get to his apartment according to the GPS on my phone. By the time I drove back home, I would miss the Christmas Eve service completely. Aunt Sheila might turn the service into a prayer vigil, fearing the worst. So as soon as I found a parking space, I sent her a text.

I wasn't able to make it to church. Sorry. I'll explain when I get home.

I hugged the package to my chest to protect it from the damp air as I searched for apartment #114. The porch light was on. White Christmas lights outlined the door.

He's home.

I approached the door with my mind ping-ponging between fear and release, my heart thumping so fast that I thought he might find me passed out on his welcome mat in the morning. Still, I managed to crouch down, lay the package on the mat, and stand.

I rang the bell and hurried away, wishing I could be there when Jason opened the anonymous package and saw the ceramic *Grace* cross, the card filled with verses, and the words on the envelope: *You're forgiven.*

Aunt Sheila sat at the kitchen table with her hands around a Santa mug. The tree lights were on and her favorite radio station's 48 Hours of Christmas was playing. She had changed into her slippers but still wore her red sweater that shimmered when light hit it.

She sprang from her chair when she saw me. "There you are. Where've you been? When I saw your text, I figured the party ran late, but I drove past the hotel on my way home and saw most of the lights off."

"Sorry I missed church."

"That's okay. Did you go out with Lydia to do something afterward?" She came over to me. "Your eyes are red. You've been crying. What happened?"

"I'm fine." I smiled. "Really, I am. I'll tell you all about it later."

She looked me over. "If you say so."

"How was church?"

"Beautiful. The bell choir played, and the worship team performed a song that made me cry so hard that I can't even remember the name of it. Good thing the choir had already sung, otherwise I would've been a mess up there. And I saw Steven."

"Steven?"

She swatted my arm. "Don't give me that. He is good-looking, you have to admit it."

I allowed myself a laugh. "Yes, he is." She wanted so badly for me to be happy. "But to be honest, he's not my type."

She ushered me to the table. "Do you have someone better in mind?"

"Actually, I think I do."

"Really? Someone has been keeping secrets."

"This is kind of a new thing."

Her whole face lit up. "Did you meet someone at the Dickens dinner?"

"Sort of."

"Tell me."

"Not quite yet." I didn't want to jinx it.

"Oh, fine, be that way. But I will get it out of you by the New Year." She patted the tabletop with her fingertips. "Sit down. I'll get you some cocoa."

"I need your help with something first."

I reached into my tote bag to retrieve Jason's package.

Aunt Sheila put her hand over her lips. "You didn't send it back."

I shook my head.

"Would you like me to wrap it up pretty for you?"

I looked down at the box in my hands. Jason had probably opened my gift by now. "No."

"What do you need from me, honey?"

I sat on the couch near the tree and patted the other cushion. "Sit with me while I open it."

She came over and sat next to me, not saying anything. I carefully picked at the tape until it came loose. From ages twelve to twenty, I looked forward to Jason gifts more than any others, but tonight I didn't care what was inside as much as the peace I had in letting go of hating him.

Under a layer of tissue, I found a bubble wrap-covered red box. I lifted the lid and the Styrofoam and uncovered a pearly jewelry box with a painting of ice skaters on the lid. I'd admired one just like it in a store the night we saw *Scrooge*.

"How lovely." Aunt Sheila touched one of the skaters.

"I wanted this. I never said anything. I knew we couldn't afford it, but I couldn't stop looking at it." I lifted the lid. The one I remembered played "Winter Wonderland." The first notes of that song barely rang out before I gasped and almost dropped the jewelry box.

A ruby bracelet sparkled against the black velvet lining.

"Oh, Justine."

I touched it to make sure it was real, examining the stones, the diamond flecks, and swirly etchings on the chain. "How did he get it back?"

It would be impossible after selling it to an antique dealer.

"I imagine the two of you have a lot to talk about, don't you?"

55

I searched for a note. I checked under the flaps of the packing box and every inch of the wrapping.

Aunt Sheila caught my hands. "Honey, doesn't the gift speak for itself?"

"I guess it does."

I took the bracelet out of the jewelry box, aching to put it on but unable to take my eyes off of it. Did he replace Mom's china, too? Obviously, she'd forgiven him with or without it.

I rested my head against my aunt's shoulder. She wrapped her arm around me.

"Just so you know, you aren't the only one who has had a hard time letting go of the past."

"You too?"

"Oh, yeah." She kissed the top of my head. "Feels freeing to let go, though, doesn't it?"

I nodded. "I forgave him before I opened the present."

"I kind of sensed that."

"So, I've been thinking. Do we have room for one more guest for Christmas dinner?"

Author Bio

*J*eanette Hanscome is the proud mom of two grown sons and the author of five books, including *Suddenly Single Mom: 52 Messages of Hope, Grace, and Promise* and *Running with Roselle* (co-authored with blind 9/11 survivor Michael Hingson). She regularly contributes to Guideposts' *All God's Creatures* devotional, in addition to writing for *Mornings with Jesus 2019, One-Minute Daily Devotions,* and several other collections. She recently returned to her love of fiction after several years of writing nonfiction. Jeanette is passionate about sharing stories of God's faithfulness and grace that highlight deep relationships. When she isn't writing, speaking at writers conferences, and coaching authors, Jeanette gravitates toward all things creative, including singing, knitting, crocheting, and art. Her new best friend is her Kala concert ukulele.

Visit Jeanette's website and blog: jeanettehanscome.com